Flavors For Friends

By Julie Ann Fairley

Amazing Short Stories and Poetry For Children

Illustrated by Lashon T. Hollington
and designs by Andrae A. Givans

Power House Media International LLC

New York, London

SAN: 858-348X

www.PowerhousePublication.com

Designed by Power House Media International LLC

Photo of author by Jerry Jack

Art Directions by Andrae Givans

Manufactured by Power House Media International LLC

www.phmillc.com

Printed in USA

FIRST EDITION

Library of Congress Cataloging-in-Publication Data

ISBN 978-0-9840750-0-3

Dear Miss Annabelle, Hope you enjoy the book! I wish you the best for the future! Happy Reading! Ms. Julie Ann Fairley

Dedication

I must say…Thank You, Thank You! Thank you all for having the God presence inside of you that allowed you to believe that I could do it. You asked and you pushed ever so gently. You nudged a bit harder when you realized that I hadn't spoken about my writing in quite some time. You didn't stop inquiring or reminding me about it from time to time. You simply asked, "Where's the book?" During the long run, during my long wait for the right words or the right sentence, I'd involved myself in an assortment of endeavors, most of which had nothing to do with "the book." Each day I went to work, to the gym, visited relatives, hung out with girlfriends. I supported my family during times of trouble. I healed from a whole lot of situations. I wrote, directed, and produced class plays for my students. All the while, as I washed a dish or took a shower or involved myself in any of the above, there was tugging at my very essence, "the book, the book, where's the dagnabbit book?"

Well…it was in huge green containers, plastic Gap bags, on sheets of lined yellow paper, tiny spiral notepads, three ring binders, and written on the inside covers of other books. "The book" was everywhere and each of you experienced pieces of it. Each of you knew, and I knew all too well about what happens to people who are not able to fulfill their dreams. Therefore, letting myself down and letting you down was not an option. More than anything in the world, I knew that I had found my greatest sense of peace and joy when I was able to write something that would enlighten and or affect change in the world.

I believe that each of us has a gift. When we acknowledge and accept our gift we are able to achieve great things. You recognized mine! Thanks to my girl, **Tawnia McCray** who came up with strategies for me to get the task done. You just jumped in and told me what I needed to do. Tawnia, I was listening! Even when you rolled your eyes and looked the other way when I gave the reasons for not having finished, I knew I had to get it together. You all know who you are. You encouraged and supported me at Open Mic events, listened to me test out a piece of writing on the phone, cheering me on. It was "fuel for the fire inside of me." It's coming, you all…I mean it! I have it; you'll see it…soon.

Well…here it is finally! ***Coco, Rainbow, Cherry, Mango Flavors For Friends, Short Stories and Poetry For Children.*** It started with the little girl inside of me who put her words on paper in Miss Travin's second grade class. The first poem is the poem I wrote when my teacher simply said, "Class… write a poem about spring." That poem, which was published in a school newspaper, was where my writing journey began. I had no idea I would revisit that place in my heart as an adult. I had no idea that an important part of my career was right within my grasp. It brings tears to my eyes…

My Auntie…My mother's only sister **Bloneva Applewhite Griffin**, who loved me from the very beginning, who listened to my poetry and simply said, "You done good Ju." Thanks Auntie for all the support, the sass and the class. I'll love you forever!

"**Aunt Penny**…**Ella Mae**," who listened as I told many a story, filling each of us with so much laughter at the end of each one. You would say, "Cut it out Ju, Stop Lyin'! I'd say, "I ain't lyin'..., for real

James Allen, my big brother, who handed me sheets of lined paper to practice my handwriting each day, (can't write anything without my yellow paper!) pages of newspaper articles to read aloud, plenty of sweet peas (ugh!!!) and all the wonderful stories about my favorite childhood television doctor, Dr. Ben Casey, who would marry me if I was a good girl. Sister loves you! **Professor Charles Bell** who once wrote on one of my college papers, "You're a poet! Know it and show it!" I thank you, Sir.

Donald Fairley, my younger brother, who told Mommy on me all the time. I know that you love me and wish me well.

Lashon…My oldest daughter who has always spewed excitement when immersed in learning something new and being creative. Your quirky drawings finally found a place in Mommy's first book. I love you!

Eyhana…My second daughter, who understood my quest tor healthy living. Thanks for all the great cards and my soy drinks. Kudos to you for teaching my grandson how important it is to sometimes give someone fresh flowers. I appreciate how you helped my grandson on a moments notice to study his lines for the poetry presentation. I love you!

Ilasia, Ilasia! Thank you youngest daughter for all of our time spent on the phone during the early morning hours. You listened to my ideas and poems. You were excited about every literary task I articulated. You gave me direction and support when I got a bit confused. Mommy loves you!

Yemi Odutola…My cool, focused younger

cousin who calls me regularly, sends me birthday cards, calls me "Gem", listens and speaks her mind. Who often uttered, "You talented Ju!" who made it her business to attend as many poetry readings that she could when I was doing a poetry reading. Love you, Girl! **Uncle B.A. (Antoine), Aunt Shalema (Reynell), Aunt Sherri**...Aunt Savasia (Bridget)You have been there from the hot kitchen to the talent shows, poetry jams and more. Love you truly.

Tiffany Phinazee Thompson... I will always be your Aunt Quani...Love Ya! **Terry and Rosalyn**...My big cousins who showed me some good times and exposed me to some serious music. From 115th Street to Linden Boulevard. I couldn't wait to get there!

Sabrina, 'briward', Ujimma...My not that much younger than me little cousin who shared a room with me along with her Cream Sodas, Coconut Cookies and Cheetos. My girl has her ***Coco, Rainbow, Cherry, Mango*** and then some going on! I love ya!!! **Patrice Ward**...Cousin, I love you. Welcome home!

Denise Damon Campbell "Auntie Bella" From 2186 to you driving four little girls in Granddaddy's Skylark, to my son's first and last day on earth; from my Dad's final day, rubbing my brother "Uncle Ron's" failing body, and my Mother... They're gone yet you touched us all. Love you all the time my "stusta."

To my sisters...Helene Gloria Butler... "Heena", from 179st until. "Ooh child, things are gonna get easier." Our love is ever present... Jeanette... "Jenny Baby" 179st on your mind, Let's stay together girl...Sallie...The first time ever I saw your face, a J.H.S.115 dream team, What! Lisa, Ramona, Barbara-Ann, Dee-Dee (Delores) Emma, Barbara-Jean, Carol, Renee ("Tudor") Gloria Denise, Rainn, Marcella, Adrienne, Shyrell, Sarah, Tanya Curtis... For every great grilled cheese sandwich on Washington Avenue, **Belinda...Edwards and Saunders!** I have you in my heart. **Applewhites and Fishburns! My Florida family**...Oh how happy you have made me!

Mr. Brian Edwards...There would never have been "Another kind of Tomorrow." Thank you, thank you my friend. **Mr. Andrae Givans**, the soft spoken,"powerhouse" who exuded patience, expertise and a willingness to "teach" me how to get the manuscript and illustrations ready for publication. Thank you My Dear...Great things are ahead of us!

My **C.S.50 family**...Love, Love, Love You!!! **Ms. Holloway**...Our outstanding librarian, whose knowledge and expertise is invaluable...Who helps me whenever I ask. Thanks for proofreading the manuscript! **Ersell Ananias**...Bold is beautiful and necessary. Sassy and stylish. Girl, Give me those shoes! Nothing but love. **Ms. Sharonda Trotman** and **Phyllis Coaxum**...I truly appreciate you and all that you do. Thanks for being right on time all the time **"Bibian"**...**Vivian Jimenez**...We are a collaborative team. Thank you for sharing and helping whatever I needed. "Julia" loves you. **Sonia Caraballo**... Thanks for your encouragement. **Carla Caraballo**... Just keep on writing because it is wonderful...Brings tears to my eyes.

Ms. Lanaya Bellamy-Grant...Girl, you always, always come through when I ask you for anything! You never hesitate and are always pleasant. I appreciate you so very much! You just don't know...**Judy Cruz**...Thanks for all your help and great ideas about one project or another.
Ms. Norman...Thank you for proofreading the work on such a short notice. ...**Cousin Rosalyn and Franz**; Thanks for being there, Love you. Thank you so much for coming to the poetry readings and coming to the J.R.P. Dances and being excited about the writing. Thank you for editing the book **Ms. Carmen Mason**.

Ms. June Carey, Ms. Cordoba...A tremendous thanks to you all for reading the manuscript and responding in a timely manner.

Dana, Dana, Dana Kirton...Us in a room, Zoom! We go there. You are so creative...Girl, we are going places. **Beverly Spencer**...For all the peace and calm, the music and the dance and wellness, Thank you. I breathe easier. **Ms. Carmen Mason**...Thank you so very much for proofreading the manuscript. You invited me into your lovely home and walked me through the work, not once but twice, helping me through my last minute jitters. I needed that tea and cookies!

Tanisha Wells...One of the first students I taught who waited by my car every day demanding to be allowed into my life. Beautiful young woman, you are in my heart. **"Auntie Fairley"** loves you!
I dedicate this book to **All** of the children and students who listened to my stories and poems. This book is for All who share in the joy and the pain. **Hey Tony Scott...J.R.P. on the move. We're on the the right track.. Keep on pushing.**

Table of Contents

Coco, Rainbow, Cherry, Mango

What flavor would you like?

A Wonderful Spring Day

Once on a spring day I saw lovely flowers,
They were so beautiful just as beautiful as can be
But the rain looked down and said "They must need me!"
The spring flowers were so happy they danced with glee
That's what happened on a wonderful spring day.

The Sound of Morning

I always loved the sound of morning,
Glory
Birds chirping, birds flying,
Soaring
Trees towering, caterpillars crawling,
Falling
Creeks flowing, rain dropping,
Pouring
I always loved the sound of the river,
Roaring
I always loved the sound of the morning,
Glory
Glory
Glory!

I CAN SEE A RAINBOW

Red and yellow and pink and green
Purple and orange and blue
I can see a rainbow, do you?
I can see a rainbow, too!

Red and yellow
Colors so alive
Pink and green
Speak softly to the eyes

Purple and orange
Are lovely any day
Blue is the color that makes me want to say,
I'm happy, I'm sad, I'm cool, I'm glad
In a funny sort of way

Yellow is the color that makes me wanna do
Some laughin' and singing and dancin' around too!
I can see a rainbow
The colors are on my mind
I can see a rainbow
With colors so alive
I'm happy
I'm sad
I'm cool
I'm glad

Want An Icee?

Ma…
Ma…
Mommy!
The hot sun is beaming
down on my face
I look up at the window
Beamin'
Burning
Making me want some-
thing
Cold, freeze
Cold to drink
Cold to slurp on
Slurp, Slurp, Slurp!
Everybody outside
pushin'
Tryin' to get to the icees
I need a quarter or a dime
and some nickels
Ching, Ching, Ching
Change!
To make my cold dream
Cold thing come true.
Ma…
Ma…
Mommy!
Stick your head
Under the shiny glass
square
Come on Ma
Come on Mommy
Hurry!
The lady with the sweet,
cold
Coco, Rainbow, Cherry,
Mango
Smooth things
Ain't gon' wait too long
For me to get my Ching,
Ching, Ching
Dimes and things
Silver and brown
Round
In my wet
Sticky hand.
Ma…
Ma…
Mommy!
I stomp my foot on the
hot ground
I yell
My throat is dry
I jump up and down
'Cause I need
Need
My cold thing
Coco, Rainbow, Cherry
Icee!
Mommy, PLEASE
Oops!
I forgot
My mind went some-
where
Empty headed girl!
Mommy ain't home
That glass up there
Is
Clear, clear
Empty!

Want An Icee?

Where Is My Homework?

You know you ain't got it

Didn't think about it

Went without it

Lost it

Could not find it

Too tired

Wasn't reminded

Left it

Little brother tore it

My sister destroyed it

Juice spilled on it

You know you just ignored it

Poetry, That's Me

I write poetry because my heart sings
Sometimes my heart aches
My soul stirs
Poetry sets me free
I write poetry when breezes are cool
When raindrops form puddles that are splashed on my legs
When raindrops tap lightly on windowpanes
When music plays
When melodies make me shiver
I am poetry in motion.
Aches, stirs, motion, FREE
Poetry, that's me
Sings – Free
Aches – Free
Stirs - Free
Cool - Free
Wet - Free
Poetry, that's me
Puddles – Legs
Window – Panes
Music - Plays
Rainy - Days
Poetry, that's me
Teardrops – Eyes
Love – Inside
Poetry, that's me

Ooday Ooryay Ingthay/ Do Your Thing

(A fun poem in Pig Latin)

Ifhay, ooyay
Auntway ootay ayplay
Umcay out today---ay
Umcay out today---ay

Ifhay ooyay
Auntway ootay ingsay
Go and do your ingthay
Go and do your ingthay

If hay ooyay
Auntway ootay anceday
Music make me oovemay
Music make me oovemay

Ifhay ooyay
Auntway ootay aughlay
Go ahead and aughlay
Go ahead and aughlay

Ifhay ooyay
Auntway to unray
Move your legs and unray
Move your legs and unray

Ifhay ooyay
Auntway ahay endfray
Be one 'til the endhay
Be one 'til the endhay

Ifhay ooyay
Auntway ootay illchay

If you
Want to play
Come out today---ay
Come out today---ay

If you
Want to sing
Go and do your thing
Go and do your thing

If you
Want to dance
Music make me move
Music make me move

If you
Want to laugh
Go ahead and laugh
Go ahead and laugh

If you
Want to run
Move your legs and run
Move your legs and run

If you
Want a friend
Be one 'til the end
Be one 'til the end

If you
Want to chill

Sit down and be illstay
Sit down and be illstay

Ifhay ooyay
Auntway ootay Icray
Let it out and ighsay
Let it out and ighsay

anceday
ingsay
Go and do your ingthay!

Icray, Unray, Ighsay, Aughlay,
Anceday, Ingsay, Endfray, Illchay

Go and do your ingthay
Go and do your ingthay
Go and do your ingthay
Ootayayday
Ootayayday
Ootayayday
TODAY

Sit down and be still
Sit down and be still

If you
Want to cry
Let it out and sigh
Let it out and sigh

dance
sing
Go and do your thing!

Cry, Run, Sigh, Laugh
Dance, Sing, Friend, Chill

Go and do your thing
Go and do your thing
Go and do your thing
Today
Today
Today
Today

Pig Latin is a twist of English for anyone who wants to be silly or for anyone who doesn't want someone to know what they're talking about. When words begin with a single consonant, remove the consonant off the front of the word and place it on the end of the word. Add ay after the consonant. Example, coat = oatcay, pen= enpay. When words begin with two or more consonants, take them off the beginning of the word, add them to the end and add ay at the very end. Scream = eamscray, thumb = umbthay. When words begin with a vowel, just add hay or yay at the end. It= ithay or ityay, orange= orangehay or orangeyay. Have fun!

RING
SING
LOVE
DOVE
ME
WE
SEE
TOY
BOY
JOY
CLEAN
BEAN
BALD
SCALD
RUDE
DUDE

Anyway

Daddy,
I loved you from the very beginning
When I realized I was me
There was you
'Cause Mommy said so.
I loved you from the very beginning
And even though
You never came by to see me
And even though
You never called me
My dreams included you
My life stories included you
And I had pictures in my mind
Of all the possibilities of you and me.
Once, I imagined you watching me jumping rope
Once, I imagined you taking me shopping
Once, I imagined you coming to my school
And once I imagined you
Picking me up and wiping my bloody face
After Lenny accidentally
Hit me with the baseball bat
Pictures in my mind
All the possibilities of you and me.
Daddy, I loved you from the very beginning
When I realized I was me,
Listening to all of Mommy's once in a while stories about you
I felt good, Anyway.
My Daddy
Knows there's me

My Daddy has to be
Busy
Very busy
And even though
You never sent me a birthday card
And even though you missed every graduation
And even though
Andre Bennett
Beat the daylights outta me in the school yard
And even though
Melvin gave me a black eye and took my money
My hopes for tomorrow included you
My prayers for better days included you
And I had pictures in my mind
Of all the possibilities of you and me.

Once, I imagined you telling those wild boys not to bother me
Once, I imagined you at the cook out
Once, I imagined you cooking breakfast
And once I imagined you picking up the phone to call me.
Pictures in my mind
All the possibilities of you and me
Daddy,
I loved you from the very beginning
ANYWAY.

Afraid

I
used to be scared
afraid of
the night
and sounds that were
not familiar
when Mommy wasn't home

I
used to be afraid
scared of
the kids who chased me
and laughed at me
just because
they could

I
used to be frightened
afraid of my own thoughts
afraid of the places they might
lead me

afraid
I couldn't get out of my own
skin

I
used to be
a lot of things
One day I changed my mind
I decided to be what I wanted
to be
Afraid
I don't have anymore time

The Park

It was sunny and bright and the park was crowded. The sprinkler was on and the little kids jumped up and down, screaming. They screamed because they were having a good time. Some mothers sat nearby watching the little ones closely. Girls were jumping rope, while others were sitting on swings, pushing their legs in and out, in and out. I could hardly wait for my turn! A little boy swung a plastic bat as hard as he could and hit a grounder. Old man Louie, with his long white pony tail was shaving ice from a huge, clear block. When he finished, he was going to put that hand- made snow into a cone-shaped cup and pour any kind of flavored syrup you wanted on it. It only cost fifty cents and for ten cents more you could have another flavor. I usually asked him to mix grape and orange for me. Sometimes he poured so much syrup in it, it ran over the sides of the cup. I slurped quickly but couldn't stop it from spilling all over my tee-shirt. The sweet juice was so, so good! Anytime you saw Old man Louie, you knew there was going to be a long, long line. Sometimes the line was too long. So today, I decided I'd eat ice-cream. Everything in the park seemed okay, but it really wasn't.

The park was my favorite place, next to Auntie's. It was my second home. There was always something to do. Each time I got the chance to go outside and play, that's where I'd go. It didn't matter if it rained or snowed. It didn't matter if it was cloudy and freezing outside, it was my place to be. I always found something to do. I climbed the Monkey Bars, played Hopscotch, rode the see-saw, watched the big boys play basketball, jumped rope, sat underneath the sprinkler, drew gigantic pictures on the ground with my chalk, and most of all, I laughed and played with my friends. I could always be found in the park right next to my school, P.S.140.

Things were different today because all of my friends went on a bus ride to Coney Island. I didn't go because Mommy didn't have enough money. Just before she went out she gave me some change for an ice-cream cone from Mister Softee. After that I walked over to a "just got empty swing" and sat down.

Right outside the park fence was a group of kids I'd never seen before. They were laughing, pushing, and shoving each other real hard. They entered the park. I didn't see anyone behind me, but all of a sudden I felt a very hard shove in the middle of my back. It was so hard that I stumbled off the swing and dropped my ice-cream cone. I turned around and saw a very tall girl with long curly hair, laughing. She laughed so loudly! Her friends were laughing too.

I stood up and yelled, "What did you do that for? I wasn't bothering you! I don't even know you!"

Somebody in the group hit me in the head with a water balloon. As I grabbed my head, the girl who pushed me out of the swing just started swinging her arms and punching me. She hit me so hard and fast that I didn't even know where the next punch was com-

ing from. All I knew was that somebody else was behind me pulling my hair. Suddenly a burst of dirt was in my face. Oh my goodness, now I couldn't see!

I wasn't screaming or yelling. I was really trying to fight back. It was just that my punches were not making a difference. There were too many kids surrounding me. Plus, that instigator was a much better fighter than me. As she beat my body and yanked me from side to side I was praying that she would stop. My face was stinging and I realized she must have scratched some of my skin off.

I heard the loud bam of a car door not too far away. Then a huge bearded man pushed himself through the crowd. He started grabbing and pulling everyone away from me. Two of the girls flew into the silver fence near the swings. The girl who clawed me had her fingers wrapped around my hair. The man grabbed her hand and twisted her wrist and boy did she scream!

"Get off me! Get off me, Mister!

He paid no attention to her until he saw I was free.

"Don't make no sense what y'all did to this girl! I watched the whole thing from my car. This girl was sittin' on the swing eating her ice-cream and you snuck up behind her and pushed her off. Then your doggone friends gonna come and jump all over this girl for nothing?"

"How you know it was for nothing?" she yelled. "You need to mind…get off me, Mister, get off me!"

"Get off you? I'm gonna hold you right here and let you see what it's like when somebody bigger than you gets the best of you. I'm gonna let you find out right now who your friends are. None of the rascals that came with you are goin' to do anything! You're just a bunch of cowards. Look at 'em running, look at 'em! I'm gonna keep you right here and let this girl whip your behind like she in a boxin' ring. I dare anybody, anybody to jump into this!"

The girl tried to wiggle away from the man but she couldn't move. Her eyes were popping out of her head and she started crying. "Mister, Mister…I ain't gon' fight her! I'm sorry."

"Sorry," he said. "Sorry! D' you see what you and your friends did to her? Just look at her face! D' you think her mother is gonna want to hear that you're sorry when she looks at her child's face, Huh? Huh?"

I stood nearby looking at her. Tears ran from my eyes and burned my cheeks and my nose. Every single space on my face was on fire.
I couldn't stop crying and my face wouldn't stop burning because it was raw!

I wanted my mother! I wanted my Auntie! I was so miserable and scared even though the man was there, protecting me. As bad as I wanted to pull her hair out, I didn't. As bad as I wanted to kick her right in her stomach, I didn't. I stared into her eyes for a few seconds. Then I just turned around and walked out of the park.

For Meechee (Michelle)

Pretty girl

With the big brown eyes

They talk

Brown eyes

They dance

Lashes that flutter

You bat them and you don't even know it.

Lashes that move

Pretty girl

With the big brown eyes

Sees it all

Sunshine

(For Tawnia McCray)

Hey!

You are sunshine

You light up the world

You make me smile during dark days and cold nights

You make me warm.

Sunshine

Sunshine

Shine!

Yeah, He's My Friend

Yeah,
He's my friend
He's silly and some might call him bad
Yeah,
He's my friend
He's crazy
There's some who he makes mad
Yeah,
He's my friend
He fights and stays in trouble too
But when I say I need him,
There's nothing he won't do
When I don't have any money
Or any place to go
He'll hang around with me
And share what he has too.
He doesn't always do his homework
Sometimes he does tell lies
We sometimes get in trouble
But that comes as no surprise
Yeah,
He's my friend

My Animal
(For Lawrence)

My animal is friendly
My animal is rough
It doesn't ask for anything
I don't give it much.

It's lots of different colors
It's kind of fuzzy too
There's two black dots in its head
That stare right at you.

My friendly, fuzzy
Wuzzy, wuzzy
Colored bubby
Is just enough
So I hold it
Then I rub it
And I'm glad that it is STUFFED!

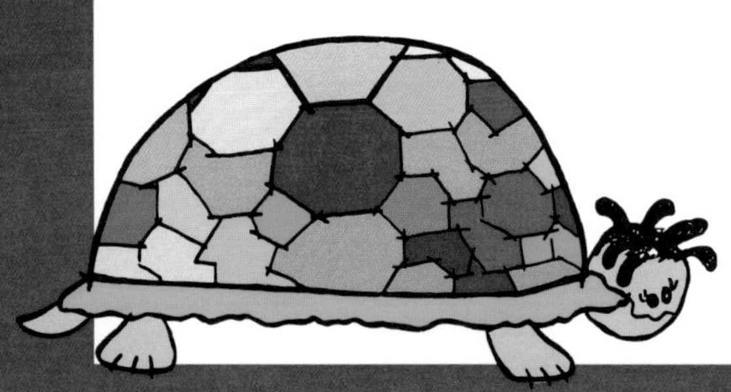

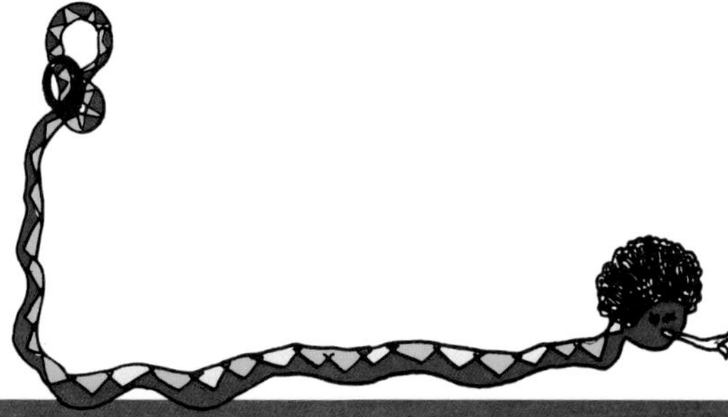

My Name Is…

I wanted a different name! I wanted to be named Terry or Barbara or Kelly. Anything except what everyone called me. Nobody I knew had a name like mine. I was the only little brown skinned girl in my whole school named Julie. The name given to me quite some time ago was Julie Ann Fairley.

I asked Mommy why she named me that plain old name. She started laughing and tried to make me feel better by saying my father called me his "Julie Poolie" when he laid eyes on me after I was born. She said as I grew up, each time he said it, I'd jump up and down and was filled with laughter. That alone was enough to let her know that she made the right choice for her queen. I smiled a little when she told me the story, but I really wasn't in a "goo-goo, ga-ga"mood. Then Ma started telling that she named me after my father's sisters. One was named Julia and the other was named Annie. (He also had sister named Alma and I was so glad she didn't give me a third name!)

Mommy named me after two women that I never, ever got to see. I never even heard their voices. Why were they so doggone important? I guessed it was because they were his sisters and she was in love with my Dad.

I tried to get her to change it. She said she wouldn't. I even started telling my friends to call me a different name. I became Dora, Toni, Dionne, and Laney.

As time went on, I finally decided that no matter what her reasons were, she had the love of family in her heart and mind when she named her only baby girl.

The Gifts I Wished I Had

Quite some time ago I wanted a pair of the latest boots for Christmas. They were really cool looking boots that came in different colors. I wanted them in white. Everybody had them and I wanted some real, real bad.

I knew that Mommy wasn't going to get me any white boots. She said I was too wild and I didn't know how to take care of things. She also said she wasn't paying all her hard earned money for some white boots I would have all dirty and torn up in no time. "Stop asking me. I told you 'no' and I mean 'no.' Ask me again and I'm gonna knock the mess out of you!"

I begged and begged anyway. Every morning I got up and went down the hall and stood by her bedroom door. She would yell, "Girl, go ahead now and get away from my door. I said 'no!' I sadly walked away.

On Christmas morning I got up and ran to the Christmas tree. There were boxes and bags of stuff, but there was no big box for me. I was pushing and grabbing gifts from my brothers. When I got to mine, it was a small box wrapped in gold paper.

Inside was a black box holding my birthstone ring and a watch with a huge, flowered face on it. I was mad, mad, mad! Mommy sat nearby explaining it was time I had some jewelry and a watch. She also said that she would be looking to see how I took care of the things she had bought.

Well, I didn't take care of that ring or that watch my mother spent her hard earned money on. I lost them and I didn't give it a care in the world until many years later…

My mother suddenly passed away one Saturday morning. All I could think of was the birthstone ring and watch she bought me that Christmas so long ago. I realized she wanted me to have something that would last longer than those white boots. Right now, I'd give almost anything, anything to have that gold ring with the clear, purple stone and the watch with the roses on its face.

The Old House

On just about any day, somebody had something to say. They'd say something, anything! If it wasn't about having ugly hair, it was about living in a raggedy house. If it wasn't about the house, it was about having a retarded brother. If it wasn't about my little brother, it was about me having a white man as my father. They made that up just because Martin, the owner of the house, lived there too. Ooh, they made me sick!

The house was
Old
Ugly
Dusty brown and dark green
Wooden
Lots of splinters
No heat
No hot water
Baths in tin tubs
With water heated on the stove.
Coal burning
No oil heat, sometimes no gas
Smoke coming straight from the grate on the living room floor!
The house was
Laughed at and pointed at and wondered about each and every day
I walked through
Squeaky gates
Quickly
Everyone knew
Mostly everyone laughed
Pointing at me
Old, ugly
Dusty brown and feeling blue
I walked quickly

What did they expect from me? It wasn't my house! I didn't buy it! I woke up one day and realized I was only half me. Me, with my own thoughts and me with my own feelings. But I also realized I was 653 East 163rd Street, corner of Cauldwell Avenue because that's what the kids saw. That's what everybody saw. I always heard something from somebody. Didn't matter if they were old or young, they pointed at the house, then me, then whispered to one another as they passed me by. Me, an eleven year old girl in the fifth grade. I had long brown skinny legs, round brown eyes and ashy knees. My ears weren't even pierced. My hair was thick, black and unruly. That's what Mommy said. The kids teased me about that too! Sunny said, "Your hair don't take water like mine does. See, mine's nice and wavy." I looked at hers, staring real hard to see how our hair was different. Hers was shorter, it smelled like peaches, because she put Dixie Peach Hair Grease in it and her hair was thick too! But I didn't see how it was better than mine. Mine was way, way longer than hers. Mine just didn't have the bangs, barrettes, rubberbands and ribbons hers had. Mommy said that I couldn't put any rubberbands in my hair because they would break off my hair. I knew how to braid my hair because my cousins, Terry and Jan, showed me how on one of their doll's heads. I practiced almost every day. I stood in front of the huge bedroom mirror with the big black comb and worked on parting my hair straight. I took my time. The perfect rectangle-shaped boxes made me smile, and the braids were "perfecto." Sunny didn't know what she was talking about, because I was working on some good hair too. That was the only thing I could work on because the old house was way, way, bigger than me!

One day, after looking at my birth certificate on Mommy's dresser, I decided I would tell the teacher that I had moved. A few minutes after I had walked into Miss Travin's class and began copying the work from the blackboard, I raised my hand. The whole class was quietly at work. I could see the teacher glaring at me over the top of her cat-shaped glasses. After a few seconds she said, "What is it young lady?" I thought, Here's the chance for me to set everybody straight! I'm going to tell her, then everybody will know I moved and stop bothering me. Everybody will know I moved to 1306 Chisholm Street, apartment 1E. Yep, that's it! That's the address on my birth certificate and that's what I'm going to say!

My heart was thumping, thumping, thumping and I was excited and nervous all at the same time. Then I said, "I need to tell you something Miss Travin." She placed her glasses on her book and said, "What is it Alodie?" I got up from my seat and went to her desk. When I got there I said, "We moved last night!"

[illegible] ook of surprise she sat up straight and said, "Moved where?"

[illegible] hisholm Street, with my father. I don't live across the street anymore."

[illegible] as I said that, the whole class had stopped working and set their eyes [illegible] see Sunny's big mouth wide open and could feel Laurie's dark eyes [illegible] in my face. I couldn't stand them! Why couldn't they just mind their [illegible] and leave me alone? My stomach started to sink. I knew I was in trouble. I couldn't even say what we always said when we lied or fooled someone about something. "Psyche! Psyche your mind!" wouldn't come out of my mouth. It was too doggone late to change my story. You don't psyche the teacher or any grown up. Miss Travin would not think it was funny at all!

"Alodie…I'm going to be sorry to see you leave us. You've been in the school since kindergarten." She lifted a red book out of one of the desk drawers, flipped the pages and began crossing out the old address and asked me to repeat the new one. Then she said, "Young lady, you're going to have to attend a new school. You live much too far away to attend P.S.140."

"No I don't, Miss Travin!" I exclaimed. "My mother said I could stay here."

"I'm afraid it doesn't work that way my dear. You are out of our district now. You have to attend your zoned school. Your mother will have to come in. In the meantime, today will be your last day here. I have to hand the transfer papers into the office. Go back to your seat now."

Transfer papers? Zoned school? What was she talking about? Oh Boy! I had just gotten myself into something. Oh well, I thought. I'll figure it out later.

I didn't realize how fast later would come. I sat miserably in my seat. Each time I looked up from my notebook or reached inside my desk for something I could see somebody's eyes. Sunny threw a balled up piece of paper at me. I pretended not to see it. Then she asked Laurie to pass me a note. I didn't feel like reading her stinkin' note. I already knew what was in it, but I took it anyway and put it underneath my notebook and acted like I was sharpening my pencil. Before I knew it she had Melanie pass me another one. Oh Boy! I wished all of them would leave me ALONE! I took the note, then lifted my notebook to get the other one. I opened the first one. It said, "YOU ARE A LIAR!" in big letters. The second note said, " LIAR! LIAR! LIAR! You ain't move nowhere. I'm goin' home with you after school to see. You gon get in TROUBLE!"

By the time I finished reading the notes my stomach was all scrambled up. I was just one gigantic bad feeling sinking deeper and deeper into itself. The feeling was worse than anything I had ever felt before. When the bell rang at 3:00 I slowly packed my books and things. I could see Sunny, Melanie, even that stupid Marvin Erilite talking and looking at me. They were all racing to get on line just as I got another idea!

I decided to be the last one out of the class. Instead of going out of Exit 7, the usual exit, I was gonna go out of Exit 5, the Eagle Avenue side. Then instead of walking home on the 163rd Street Cauldwell Avenue side, I would take a long, slow walk towards 149th and 3rd Avenue. Sunny and them wouldn't wait that long for me, because she had to be home before her big sister Rae got there. She wouldn't go knocking on my door because she knew my mother never let me have company. Besides, they said that the house was haunted and they were all scared of it and all scared of Martin, the old German man who sat in the yard every-day. He had long, white hair, whiter than his skin. He wore brown, crooked, held-together-with- tape -glasses. His shoes were big black , flip floppin' shoes with the front toes cut out. Martin's ankles were red and swollen, because Mommy said he had an illness called "Gout." The gout thing also had his fingers all twisted too. He walked with a cane. He didn't even speak the same way, well he did, but it just sounded different. That's because he was German. To me, he was kind of Santa Clausy, and he often looked out for me and my three little broth-ers when Mommy was not at home.

Every time the kids started trying to hang around the house he banged his cane on the flaky, green fence and chased them away. He didn't always chase them away. Some of them started swinging on the gate like it was something to ride on. Martin had made me a nice swing in the front yard. I used to sometimes let Sunny and Isadora ride it, but they started bringing some really bad kids that lived in their building with them. Those kids threw rocks and spit on me. They even threw soda cans they got out of the garbage at me. For what? Why were they so awful? When they weren't doing that, they were cursing and saying all sorts of mean and nasty things about me that weren't even true! "Gettaway from here! Gettaway from here, you rascals!" The whole time Martin was bangin' on the gate. What made it worse was that he didn't have any bottom teeth and the four that he did have were honey brown.

Those kids swore he was my father. "How's he my father?" I'd ask. " Look at me and look at him!" Then someone would say, " Well...he's your grandfather then." Angrily I'd yell, "You all are so stupid!"

Well that day I hoped and prayed that Martin, my so-called father, my so-called grandfather, Martin, who owned the raggedy- behind house we lived in was sitting in the yard. Yeah, I could just picture my nosey, so called friends, quickly running away!

Before I left the classroom, Miss Travin asked me to put all my books on top of my desk. She allowed me to keep the workbooks, but the hard covered books had to stay. Once again she said she was sorry to see me go. This time I just nodded my head and slowly walked toward the door. Once there, I stood in the doorway pretending to look around the classroom for the last time. I was really looking down the hall to make sure I didn't see Sunny or anybody else. Nobody was there, Exit 7 was clear. I was free to leave. I waved good-bye to my teacher and closed the door.

As I walked down the hall I put my hand on the cold blue wall bricks. They were smooth and shiny. Right then I realized I loved my school. How was I going to go to another school? I didn't even know how to get to my father's house. What made it worse was I barely remembered him! I had seen him very early one morning when I was six years old. I had gotten up to use the bathroom and he was sitting in the living room talking to Mommy, smoking a cigarette. His hair was white and wavy and he had a white moustache. I didn't even know who he was, but there was something about him that was familiar. Mommy said, "Alodie …Come here for a minute and say hello to your father. He's gonna come back and take you shopping." When she said 'father,' I was the happiest little girl with a great big smile!

Five years passed by and he never came by again. I never went shopping with him either. Every time I asked about him, Mommy would get angry and tell me to stop asking. "Go somewhere and sit down!" she'd say.

I wasn't angry at my father, but that awful sinking feeling showed up each and every time I thought about him. I didn't even care about the new clothes anymore. I just wanted to see myself outside of the mirror I loved to be in front of. Mommy would say on a good day, "Girl the older you get, the more you look just like Sparky!" Or she would say, "Your father walks around just like you do eating apples. You got that from him." She had such a calm look on her face, and she made him sound so nice. Then she'd start talking about how well he used to take care of us when I was a baby. "That man used to come home from work and look in the refrigerator and make sure there was enough food. When there wasn't, he used to put money right on the kitchen table so I'd be able to go and get some. He made sure all the bills were paid. I didn't have to worry about that."

I thought, How could a father who did all of those good things once upon a time, not make sure his only daughter had good shoes on her feet? The soles of my Penny Loafers were flappin'. I walked on one of them like I was skiing. When I didn't do that, I often tripped when I walked or my shoe would come off and my sock would show, all raggedy and torn. Why? Well, I dragged it and ragged it and tucked it back in! Just one more thing for people to talk about. It was terrible. Oh Well…I would have to ask somebody how to get to that address on my birth certificate. But today I was gonna take my long walk down to 149th Street and 3rd Avenue and hang out in Alexander's Department Store for a little while. Then I would take my bad feelings inside myself home. I had no idea how long I would feel awful. I did know that I was in the beginning of a whole, whole lot of trouble!

Daddy,
I loved you from the very beginning
When I realized I was me
There was you
'Cause Mommy said so.
I loved you from the very beginning
And even though
You never came by to see me
And even though
You never called me
My dreams included you
My life stories included you
And I had pictures in my mind
Of all the possibilities of you and me
Once I imagined you watching me jump rope
Once I imagined you taking me shopping
Once I imagined you coming to my school
And once I imagined you
Picking me up and wiping my bloody face
After Lenny accidentally
Hit me with the baseball bat
Pictures in my mind
All the possibilities of you and me
Daddy
I loved you from the very beginning
When I realized I was me
Listening to all of Mommy's once in a while
Stories about you
I felt good anyway.
My Daddy
Knows there's me
My Daddy has to be
Busy
Very busy
And even though
You never sent me a birthday card
And even though
You missed some important things
And even though
Andre Bennett
Got the chance to
Beat the daylights outta me
In the school yard
And even though
Melvin gave me a black eye and took my money
My hopes for tomorrow included you
My prayers for better days included you
And I had pictures in my mind
Of all the possibilities of you and me
Once I imagined you telling those wild boys not to bother me
Once I imagined you at the cook out
Once I imagined you cooking breakfast
And once, I imagined you picking up the phone to call me
Pictures in my mind
All the possibilities of you and me
Daddy,
I loved you from the very beginning
Anyway

I walked very fast, passing by Veronica's building, passing byDaniel's building, then down the steep hill we called, "Dead Man's Hill." It was said a few kids got killed on it by zooming their bicycles down the hill and being unable to stop and running straight into traffic. Once, Islid on the top of a broken toilet seat some kids had used as a sled. I hadan idea. When I started sliding, I rolled off sideways when it got too fast and on the ground I went. That stopped all of that speeding stuff, all of that.

"Help, help…I can't stop, Ma!" Scraped up- yes! Dead- no! I only did it one time, but I gotta say, I was scared out of my mind!

Dead Man's Hill was empty. No cars, just some garbage that had been thrown around. I saw a gray striped cat with a big bushy tail running across the street into an alley. It was lonely and it gave me a strange feeling as I passed by. It was something that made me feel worse than I already did.

All changed when I saw the gigantic blue letters that spelled out Alexander's. Obviously I didn't realize how quickly I'd gotten to Third Avenue. There were so many people going in and out of all the stores. I even got the chance to peek into Buster Brown's shoe store. I used to love climbing up into the little burgundy seats to get my feet measured when Mommy did take me to get shoes. Martin even took me one time. I loved the feel of the cold metal on my foot. Today I just went inside, right up to the seats and realized I was way too big to be sitting in those seats anymore, way too big.

I also realized there was nothing, not one pair of shoes in the window or the store that I liked. Oh well, no more lollipops for me. Mommy was going to have to take me someplace else for shoes. That wasn't going to be hard. There were lots of other shoe stores down the block. There was Miles, National and Fred Braun. I decided to go look at shoes.

The huge shiny glass windows had everything, every beautiful shoe you could imagine behind them. Some were black, brown, suede and leather. Some were square toed, some were round toed. Others had straps across them with large and small heels. They were so nice. I saw a shiny, black patent leather pair with a small silver buckle on the front that I fell in terrible trouble that was following my behind. I hurried back down the block accidentally bumping into people along the way.

Ooh, please, I thought. Mommy, please buy them for me along with the chocolate suede round toed ones with the chocolate shoe laces. I saw a cool pair of black Hush Puppies and some Converse sneakers. I could imagine myself in each pair. I saw all the dresses, shirts, socks and barrettes I'd wear. I had spent a lot of time looking in magazines in Mr. Jeff's Candy Store, so I knew about all of the pretty colors kids wore. But it was all in my mind, along with all of the terrible trouble that was following my behind. I hurried back down the block accidentally bumping into people along the way.

Alexander's was a great place to be. I knew a lot about where things were because I sometimes went inside with Sunny and her big sister Rae. It was a whole new world. A world where I, Alodie, was the cutest, smartest, best dressin' girl in the whole school. Oops! Couldn't forget to try on some jewelry or smell all of the wonderful perfumes. It was almost dark when I left the store. I felt a stomach dip that made me want to throw up! Trouble, trouble, triple trouble. I was in deep. My mother was going to be, as she would say, "mad as hell!" I could just imagine her saying, "Girl, where have you been?" She'd be talking through her teeth. Next thing she'd say, "Alodie, get in here before I break your neck!" She'd start yelling and her mouth would be all twisted as she pointed toward the rickety, crickety door. Oh boy! The twins would be standing nearby, their eyes popping out of their faces. Ronald would have his thumb in his mouth standing behind Ma. He'd be the first to ask me a gazillion questions. "Where you been Alodie? Why you ain't take me?" Those two questions were always the first. "I can't take you everywhere I go! You're too little and too slow." He never liked my answer and would stand beside me just to show how tall he was next to me.

She always asked me where I'd been, because most of the time I was not where I was supposed to be. I loved the park and I loved playing with my "sometimey" friends. They lived in the Forest Projects. When they weren't making me feel like garbage they were lots of fun to be with. We got ourselves into all kinds of stuff. We visited a whole lot of places we didn't have permission to be. When we were behaving we hung out in the projects. We ran through the huge colored concrete barrels, climbed the rocks or roller skated down the hill in our Super Skates. Fun, fun, fun! We played tag, hot peas and butter, and RCK! Run, Catch, Kiss was a lot of fun if you liked somebody. That game was no fun if one of the not- so- cute boys decided to choose you. Anytime a boy I didn't like played the game I always found something else to do like, "Let me go see what my mother wants!" Wasn't no ugly boy gon' be kissin' on me! That would just be something else for my friends to laugh and talk about. When I was on their good side I could do no wrong. When they felt like that, all I wanted to do was to stay and play with them.

Oh boy! How I wished I was on their good side today. I tip-toed up to the gate and slowly pushed it open. I didn't want the squeaky sound of the rusty hinges to make noise. Mommy always paid attention to the noises she heard in the yard. Plus, I wasn't home yet, so I knew she'd be listening for a sign of me. Now, what was I going to tell her?

Mommy didn't hear me come into the yard, so I tip-toed right up to the front window. I peeked through the glass. I saw her switching the channels on the television set for the twins. I was stuck staring at a woman I knew would be turning into Frankenstein as soon as she saw my face! There would be no "Come on in baby…" Nobody would be glad to see me except Ronald and Donald. Just what in the world was I going to say to her? I got an idea! Nothing! I decided to just look stupid and say nothing. My punishment would be quick. She'd probably bop me right in the center of my forehead with her wooden spoon, then question me like the police on television do to their captured suspects. One thing was for sure… she would be so, so, so angry at me. More like angry to the tenth power. Angry times angry times angry times… She'd probably say something like, "Go get outta my face before I end up in jail!" I closed my eyes tightly and prayed. I prayed she would have "mercy on my soul!" I needed her to feel sorry for me. Grandma always said that and she seemed to be all right. Yeah, I needed some mercy on my soul. If mercy could be picked up, I needed enough to fit into a great big laundry bag. A gigantic, super-duper-sized load of mercy. I thought,

Mommy, Mommy
Have mercy on me!
Have mercy on me!
Your baby,
Your baby,
Your only, your only
Baby girl!

Oh Well… There was no more time to hang outside peeking through the window. Either Martin would come out from his side of the house and start yelling my name or somebody else who knew me would say something like, "Why you peeking through the window?" Somebody was always, always good for minding someone else's business! On the count of three, I was just going to have to put my key in the door, turn the lock and PUSH! Then all giggly and loud, I'd say "Hi Ma!" Then I'd run and hug the twins. Yeah…that's what I'd do. One, two, three…No sooner than I said 'three,' the wooden door seemed like it just flew open and a nose burst of green peppers and onions smacked me in the nose. Boy, I didn't even realize I was hungry until I smelled food. Ump, my favorite,- meatballs and spaghetti with hot fresh garlic bread and a nice ice-cold glass of ginger-ale! I knew that smell, and it was the only thing that made me feel a teeny bit better.

"I'm gonna break your doggone neck young lady! Don't think

you're gonna burst in here and try to fill my head up with a pack of lies. I'm going to ask you again, Alodie…before I come over there and choke you to death, where in the world have you been?" She hollered so loudly I could see a huge brownish green veins between her eyes. I was scared and miserable.

"Ma…you didn't even give me a chance to tell you anything."

Her eyes were as wide as they could stretch and her face looked like she'd been suckin' on lemons all day. I knew she was not about to stand in the middle of the living room floor patiently waiting for me to give her an answer. Something would happen and one thing was for sure: it would not be good! My plan was not going to work, so I decided to say, in the lowest possible voice, "Nowhere."

"What? she screamed. "What? Speak up Alodie before I…"

"I…said…nowhere, Mommy."

"You are three hours late from school and you have the nerve to tell me, nowhere? Have you lost your ever lovin' mind Alodie? Have you?"

She was slowly coming my way. I started backing up and I didn't answer her. Instead, I started picking at the skin on the side of my thumbnail and staring at the wooden floor. For a moment I thought the best thing for me to do to save myself would be to run! Run back outside the door into the night. I'd run to Sunny's house. I'd tell her the truth, let her punch me a few times like she usually does when she thinks I'm foolin' her. Usually she'd help me when I got in trouble because most of the time, when she wasn't being a show off, she was with me. A couple of times we told her mother that my mother had to take the twins downtown to my aunt's house and my mother said it would be okay if I spent the night. The truth was my mother was working overtime in the token booth and Martin was watching the boys. I did not want to stay in the house with them, because most of the time I was doing the watching. If Martin didn't see me, he'd come over, feed them and make sure they were fine. That story worked a few times, so for a second the thoughts in my head were about friends. I knew better though, because Sunny was mad at me. She wouldn't help me at all! I wished I could tell somebody the real, real reason for me always being gone.

There was no place for me to go, so I quickly ran behind the swivel chair. I could turn it all kinds of ways to protect myself from Frankenstein for a little while. Oh, shoot! Frankenstein was standing in the spot I just ran from and she had the worst, crunched up face I'd ever seen. She yelled, "Alodie…Alodie! I don't know what in the world I'm gonna do with you. I am sick and tired of you and your lies girl. Every time I turn around you've got some situation, some dagnabbit thing that happened that your behind is in the middle of. You're always in the middle of something, and before I go to jail, I'm just gonna put you in a home! They got places for hard headed children that don't listen to their parents. Yeah…that's what I'm gonna do if I catch you in another one of your lies. I'm gonna go down to the Criminal Courthouse and file the papers. Just gonna tell the judge why you can't live in my house anymore. Judges can't stand liars, Alodie. They lock 'em up and throw away the key. You'll be a grown woman when you get out, grown and on your own! Do you understand me Alodie? Do you hear me girl? I'm signing the papers so they'll put you in The Girls Home For Liars! It's a doggone shame I can't trust you at all. Come from behind that chair and go wash your face and hands. That's what I'm gonna do…put you away the very next time something like this happens."

I wasn't quite sure whether or not I was safe, but Ooh Wee, I could breathe. Even though my stomach had been flippin' all around, I felt better. I would be able to eat dinner, wash up, and run to bed, but I knew my problems were far, far from over.

The next day I got up early and did all of the important things before leaving the house. I emptied out all the flat ginger ale, brushed my teeth with my favorite Crest Toothpaste and washed my face in the usual cold water. There was never any hot water coming out of the faucet, because there was never any money to pay the coal bill. I hated the cold water so much so I rubbed the cloth over my face real fast. I had to make sure there were no dried crust in the corners of my eyes and no dried spit on the sides of my cheeks. Grandma once told me to make sure before I left the house, I was clean. She said it was important to take care of your "personal hygiene" and that if you could smell yourself, so could somebody else. The last thing in the world I wanted to hear was one of my fans calling me ,"Alodie the Funky Chicken!" I took the orange bar of Dial Soap and wet it. Then I rubbed it back and forth on my washcloth and wiped my face and ears. Couldn't have no caked up wax in my ears. I knew that when people looked at you, especially the ones who were around me, they looked at everything!

Oh Boy! I had to hurry up and get out of the house fast. I had to beat Sunny and them to the schoolyard. Yeah…I thought. Let them see me jumping rope with Sheila Lawson. She was always the first one in the yard with her sister. Sunny would be the first one to come up to me and start asking me a bunch of questions. The rest of the nosey crew would be tagging along like puppies, just listening waiting for something to talk about. This is what they did all day, everyday, until something else interested them.

When I reached the schoolyard, Sheila was there, her sister Lyria was there and so was Sunny. It seemed like most of my class was standing there! I started to run but then I thought, “Wasn’t I early? What time was it?”

“There she is! Sunny yelled. “You big liar! I knew you would try to beat me to school, but I fooled you, didn’t I? Hey y’all…look how stupid she looks. I told y’all she’d try to beat us here. HA! HA! HA! LIAR! So…where did you say you moved to Alodie?”

“1306 Chisholm Street for your information. What do you care? Why don’t you go somewhere and mind your big- eyed business?”

“I am minding my business! I’m fighting for …truth. Ain’t that what we learned in school? Truth and justice for all! Alodie, you know you ain’t move no doggone where, ooh!”

“Yes I…”

Just then, the loud sound of the school bell rang and just about everybody started running to line up. The teachers had come outside and were now waiting to go into the building. I was so glad to see Miss Travin. I hurried to the middle of the line, wishing that I could go in front of the line just so I’d be away from Sunny and the rest of them. At the same time I was wishing I could go to the back of the line and not be too close to the teacher. Dog, dog, dog it! I knew as soon as Miss Travin got the chance she would do the “Sunny” to me. I swear. I didn’t feel like hearing any of it.

I was about to walk inside the classroom when the teacher pulled me aside, right against the door. She allowed everyone else to enter and they began the morning routine. Why wouldn’t she just leave me alone? I thought. I was a good student, smart and hard-working. Anytime she asked me to read aloud or do anything, I obeyed. My class work and homework were always neat. Shoot, I loved school! I really, truly, sincerely loved it more than anything in the whole wide world. I could never leave P.S.140, NEVER! It was the best place with the exception of being at Auntie’s, to be.

“Alodie, Did you tell your mother that she had to come in to officially discharge you from the school?”

“Officially, Um…What do you mean? No, I just forgot. I’m going to tell her this afternoon.”

“Alodie, This isn’t a game. I’m going to send you downstairs to the office with a note. Give it to the secretary, Mrs. Westberry. She’ll call your mother and explain everything to her.”

Call my mother, Oh no! I didn’t think about anybody calling my house. I took the note and right then, Sunny, in her orange and brown polka dot dress, stood next to the teacher and asked, in the most sugary voice, “Miss Travin, May I go to the bathroom?

Miss Travin turned her heart shaped face toward Sunny and asked and answered all at the same time. "Young lady, Who gave you permission to get out of your seat? I'll tell you who did, Nobody! Now go and do what you're supposed to do. You know no one is allowed out of the room at this time."

Na, Na, Na, Na, Na! Good for her! She was just trying to make sure I saw her real good. She would have maybe followed me to the office just to let me know that she was not about to stop bothering me.

I took the note from the teacher and began to walk down the hall to Exit 3. I pushed open the door and I got a big idea! Shoot, I wasn't gonna give Mrs. Westberry any note. I would go to the second floor, walk by Mr. Kaback's office, then the main office, and finally right out of Exit 7 to the street. I would stay outside all day long. I had places to go. Third Avenue would be just fine. I'd walk up Boston Road and pass Papa Charlie's Burger Bun. Then I would stop and look in the window of the meat market. There were always two huge dead pigs hanging upside down with their cloudy blue eyes. Inside there were lots of long ox tails on a silver tray just waiting to be weighed, cut, and bagged up for somebody's meal. There were always slabs of a thick brown organ called "liver" Mommy sent me to get sometimes. Liver! I hated it but I gotta admit when she fried onions and green peppers and added the floured hunk of meat, it really smelled good!

I quietly pushed the Exit door open and held on to the outside handle. Nobody was around and I was not about to make one single sound. As soon as I closed it, I tip toed away from the building. Nobody was in sight. Cars were passing by, buses rolled down the hill, and I could smell fried bacon coming from Mr. Jeff's luncheonette as the breeze blew by. I was not about to go in that direction because if he saw me I'd become his business too!

It was a bright, beautiful day with a big yellow ball in the sky. Blue and yellow looked nice together and they were my favorite colors. It was just the two with not even one cloud. It was warm and breezy, and I was so glad I didn't need a sweater or a jacket. If I did, it would be just one more problem.

I started skipping down the hill, and walking as far away from 163rd Street as I could. Finally I made a left turn and saw people getting on and off the 29 Bus to 125th Street. Some older kids were getting on through the back door. I decided not to walk any further, because this was my chance to ride.

Yeah, riding all the way down to 149th Street would be great. I'd go window s hopping. The clothes in the stores were always the latest looks for boys and girls. The hats, bags, pants, dresses and whatever the mannequins wore had been arranged just the right way. Everything matched. Wow!

The bus driver skipped some stops and that was fine with me. I stood close to the back door. The bus was crowded and filled with a whole lot of loud talking. It was packed with high school kids. It was so hard for me to see outside, because there were so many people taller than me. When the bus came to a stop and someone got off Ooh wee, I got a space! I was now able to peek a little out of one of the windows. But what I didn't see from behind me would change my life forever! With a strong hand and long curled fingers around the back of my neck, NOWHERE was where I'd be going. Oh shoot! My stomach dropped and flipped. My heart beat quickly. It skipped and then I felt a sudden thump. Oh shoot, Jimboy!

All I Can Be

I have to be
All I can be
'Cause someone sacrificed so much for me
I have to work
As hard as I can
So the ones behind me will understand
I have to work and do
All that I can
'Cause someone before
Had a dream in their hands
I have to be
All I can be
'Cause someone who's watching may follow me
I have to listen
I have to think
I have to try
Can't give up and sink
I have to ask questions
When I am confused
Can't sit and pretend
That everything is cool
I have to look deeply
I have to decide
To do the wrong things or to do what is right
I have to take time
A few minutes each day

Be still, just listen to what my heart has to say
I have to be
All that I can
That will show
How much I love me
And when I love me
Is when I can love you
When that love is shown
There's much we can do
I have to be
All I can be

There's so much to see
There's so much that we
Can dream, (clap, clap)
Can do (clap, clap)
Can work, (clap, clap)
You too
I have to be
All I can be
All I can be
All I can be
All (clap) I (clap) can (clap) be (clap)
All I can be!

Toe Tales

Everybody in the family has different toes

Jimboy's toes are long and skinny

He has big bumps on his pinky toes...

He has corns.

Auntie V's toes are short and stubby…

She has corns on top of corns almost looking like a piece of corn…

Ooh! Look at her feet in the summer. She loves wearing white sandals and polishing her toenails bright red and putting white dots on them. Brother D, My goodness! Uncle Ron told him to change his socks but he ain't listen, so he got Whatchu call it? Whatchu call it? Athlete's feet and all his long brown toes smell like cheese and his toenails look like Whatchu call it? Whatchu call it? Sunflower seeds. And my feet, my feet

are big and pretty!

Life

Give me rocks and oceans and trees and seas
Seeds and birds that fly

Give me stars and moons and clouds and rain
Thunder that roars up high

Give me lakes and rivers and flowers and plants
Grass that's oh so green

Give me music and dance and people that sing
Life,
What a wonderful thing!

Give me sunny days or snowflakes
Give me raindrops from dark gray clouds

Give me honey dipped or ice-cream whipped
Cookies, pizza, or pie

Give me strong warm breezes and ocean scents
Wet sand right under my feet
Give me music and dance
People that sing
Life,
What a wonderful thing!

The Monste
Hear-Say

This poem, "***The Monster Hear-Say"*** was inspired by my grandfather, Caiphas Applewhite who knew a lot about the same monster long ago, and wrote about the monster also.

The Monster Hear-Say

You better watch out for that monster!
You better watch out for that monster!
Monster Hear,
Monster Say.

We're gonna tell you 'bout that monster,
We're gonna tell you 'bout that monster,

What we say
You know is true
The monster Hear-Say
Will come for you!

It makes you listen
It makes you laugh
It makes you smile
Will make you sad.

It tells you things you didn't know
Tells you stories
And how things go.

Will make you listen
Will make you smile
Will bring you trouble
In a little while.

You better watch out for that monster!
You better watch out for that monster!

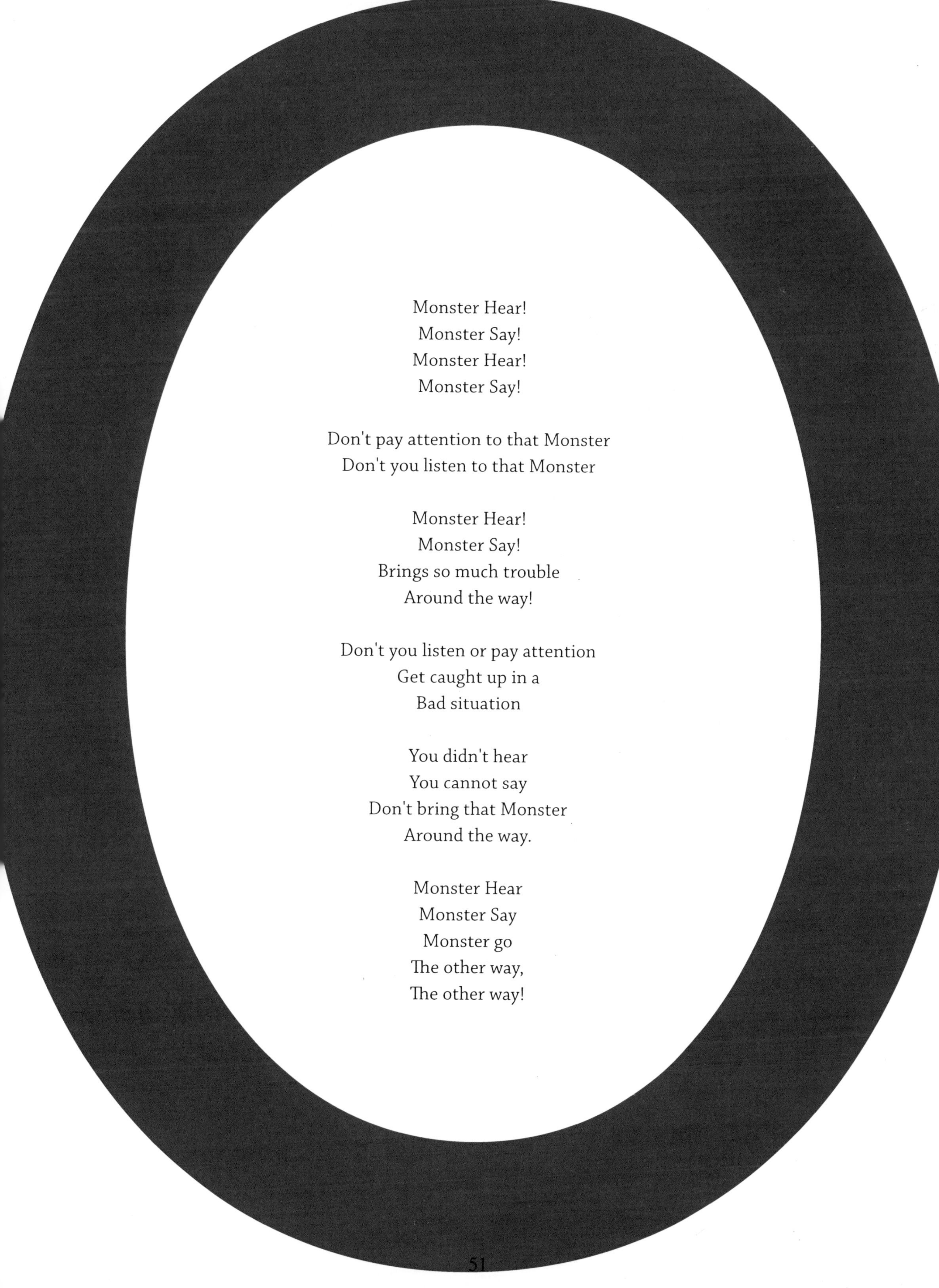

Monster Hear!
Monster Say!
Monster Hear!
Monster Say!

Don't pay attention to that Monster
Don't you listen to that Monster

Monster Hear!
Monster Say!
Brings so much trouble
Around the way!

Don't you listen or pay attention
Get caught up in a
Bad situation

You didn't hear
You cannot say
Don't bring that Monster
Around the way.

Monster Hear
Monster Say
Monster go
The other way,
The other way!

My Friend

I wanted you to be my friend
But then again
I shoulda thought about it first
Because
I really didn't know you.

I wanted you to be my friend
You were new here
I smiled and welcomed you
I shoulda thought about it first

Because
I really didn't know you.

I wanted you to be my friend
So you wouldn't have to walk home alone
I waited for you after school
Introduced you to my friends
But then again
I shoulda thought about it first
Because
I really didn't know you.

I wanted you to be my friend
So we could call each other and laugh

About TV stars and candy bars and IPods
What we were gonna wear tomorrow
But then again
I shoulda thought about it first
Because
I really didn't know you.

A friend begins deep within
It doesn't happen fast
'Cause often when it does
It really doesn't last

I wanted you to be my friend
But then again
I shoulda thought about it first
Because
I really didn't know you.

We don't talk and we don't laugh
When we see each other
Neither one of us feels good

A friend begins deep within
It doesn't happen fast
'Cause often when it does
It really doesn't last.

I wanted you to be my friend
But then again
I shoulda thought about it first
Because
I really didn't know you.

I Can't Help It

I was minding my business
Just standing alone
But the world is exciting
Like you didn't know!
There's so much to see
There's so much to tell
I can't help it if I
Can't keep it to myself.

The trees, the bees, the birds, the
flies
The lady, the man, the boys, the time
The clothes, the shoes, the cars, the
homes
Can't help it if I have to talk on the
phone!

The girls, the secrets, the games, the fun
The jewelry, the music, the cutest one
The party...Who's coming? I'm going there
too,
I'll tell you what I saw and you'll tell me too!
My cousins, my Tee-Tee, my family, my friend
My sister, my brother, my Uncle and them

I was minding my business
Just looking around
The world is exciting
Gotta share what I've found!

But I've gotta cool it
Can't be so surprised
When things go on and about in our lives.

It's hard you see

Ooh! I can't help what I say

The world is exciting
Now they're calling me NAMES!

"You're so nosey,
Shut your mouth
Got so much to talk about!"

I can't help it
Is what I say
A wonderful world
It would be a disgrace
If I wasn't able to say what I say
I just can't help it.

I'm Not The Same

I'm not the same
I'm not like you
Look at my face, my hair
My lips, my shoes

I laugh funny --- HEE, HEE, HEE!
I walk funny -----as you can see

I play around though
I like to have fun
I like music, movies, video games
And then some

I love pizza and candy
I love ice-cream and cake
I love going to parties
I love walking around
Getting wet in the rain

I'm not the same
I'm not like you
My heart's been broken
By lots of people, SHOOT!

They laugh at me because I'm different or new
They chase me and hurt me too
They try to take the money I've saved
What they don't know
Is that I work EVERYDAY!

I help Old Man Beemo
From around the block
We collect bottles and cans
He shares his stuff

In class it's hard
Sometimes I can't read
Sometimes things get mixed up
Then you laugh and you tease

Sometimes numbers, signs
Division and percent
Probability and fractions
Don't make ANY sense

My writing is a mess
The work is often hard
But Hey, That's me
I guess I'm pretty odd

I'm not the same
I'm not like you
Look at my face, my hair
My lips, my shoes

Listen to the words
Yes, my heart does speak
I try not to feel lonely
While you call me GEEK or FREAK
Or just beat me up
Whenever you can

I'm not the same
I'm not like you
Look at my face, my hair
My lips, my shoes

I stand right now
For you all to see
How my heart speaks

What's the matter with me?
What's the matter with me?

I'm not the same
I'm not like you
I look at myself and tell the truth
It's the right thing to do.

I can draw and I can paint
I fix computers when they go on the blink
I can travel alone
On buses and planes
You don't even know how many countries I've seen
You don't even know how well I can sing!

So I'm here to say once again

I'm not the same
I'm not like you
Look at my face, my hair
My lips, my shoes.

It's someone like me
Who is not the same
Who hopes they can bring about change.

It's someone like me
Who is NOT the same
Who WILL bring about change.

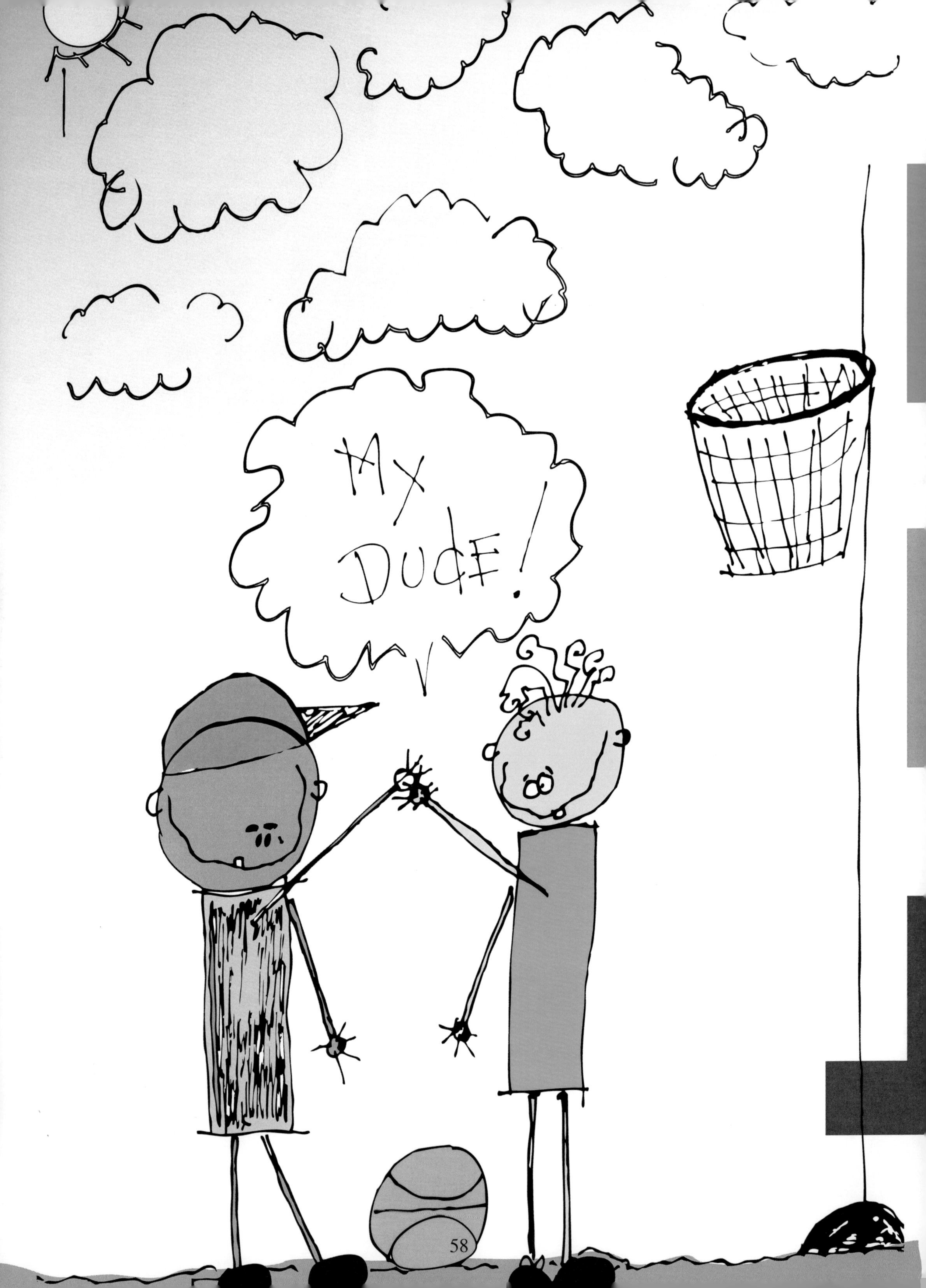
MY DUDE!

Best Friends

Rough, tough
Had enough
Stop! No!
Let me go.

Rough, tough
Knocked me down
Push and pull me all around.

Rough, tough
They don't see
You're as gentle as can be
You're so funny and we laugh
I'm so glad you're in my class!

Rough, tough
Make me mad
I am stronger
You ain't bad!

Rough, tough
Let's go see
The world together
You and me!

Around the corner,
Up the stairs
After class, ANYWHERE
Look at wrestling, basketball
Catch a football down the hall
We're just laughing having fun
All we want to do is run!

Rough, tough
I'm so glad
Best friend I could ever have,
Ever have!

He Said, She Said

You said and I said and he said, It's true
He said that she said, Yes we said it too.
They said that I said
Now that isn't right
You said that I said
Now they had a fight.

She said that I heard that he said it after
That was last week
Now what does it matter?

You said that I said and he said it's true
He said that she said
Now what about you!

This sounds so crazy,
Confusing my mind
It happens so often and all of the time.
She said and he said and they said it all
Now who said it really,
Who's really at fault?

He said and she said
What is her name?
She said that they said
Now who will we blame?

You said and I said and he said it's true
She said that he said
Now what about YOU?

The sound of silence
Gets me into my own thoughts
I want to rest
Take it easy
Do nothing except think
Close my eyes
Breathe,
Breathe,
Breathe,
Just
Take it easy

Things Are Possible

Sunshine
and
blue skies
make me
feel good
When I
feel good
so many things are
possible
yo digo
cosas es possible en mi cabeza
y en mi corazon
cada dia y cada noche

About the author Julie Ann Fairley

Photo by Jerry Jack

I am the only daughter of the late Sadie Marie Applewhite. Now I am all grown up. I was born and raised in The Bronx in the borough also known as "The Boogie Down Bronx." I am an experienced teacher and writer. In ***Coco, Rainbow, Cherry, Mango Flavors For Friends***, I revisit a few of the many experiences and lessons learned as a child.

"Julie Ann," she yelled as she stood in the front yard looking up and down the block for me. "Where in the world have you been? Who is this? What did I tell you to do in the first place? No... You can't go back outside. No... You can't have any company and no, you can't spend the night. Don't ask me if she can stay for dinner because I can barely feed you. Girl, you better go somewhere and sit down!" From what I have observed in the classroom, I have learned as much as things changed, many of the lessons are still necessary and remain the same.

There is a common thread of conflicts children experience and internalize. As a writer, I felt the need to expose myself and become the voice for some of their joy, pain and concerns. In doing so, I tapped into the little girl inside of me. I used her experience to show children when an adult says, "I do understand," there truly is some truth in their words. Julie Ann Fairley received her B.A.degree and M.S. in Education from Herbert H. Lehman College in The Bronx. She teaches elementary school in New York City and has been teaching for many years. She is the mother of three daughters and one son. You can find more information on Julie Ann Fairley at www.julieannfairley.com.

IN MEMORY

Mommy...Sadie Marie Applewhite, aka "Tootsie" my strong, outspoken, determined mother who steered me in the "write" direction when I professed my becoming an accountant, token clerk and a nurse. "You're like my father...he wrote poetry."

Granddaddy...Caiaphas Applewhite who had the courage along with Uncle "Benny" Benjamin Applewhite to write, leaving behind a road map of family history which Mommy placed in my hands.

My Dad...Angus Lee Fairley, who kept on asking me to write scriptures from the Bible on his new wallets. On the last day of his life he reached out his arms and said, "I'm sorry Baby, I love you!

Grandma, "Granny"...Mamie Edwards Applewhite, the powerful little woman who took the time to take me on bus outings, visits to family and fishing with Cousin Roscoe. She had an extraordinary amount of patience and an abundance of love for everyone.

My brother, Derek Lawrence Fairley, who was comforted by my original songs and singing long ago.

My brother, Ronald Eugene Fairley, who was with me through adversity and success, loved me unconditionally, and knew what to say to me and how to say it when necessary.

My son , S.Nakwanne Hollington, who ate cheese doodles between my knees as I wrote, wrote, wrote!

My one and only Auntie, Mommy's only sister...Bloneva Applewhite who called me her "Gem" and showered me with nothing but love and goodness.

And my Beautiful, "sister" Beverly Ann Thompson whom I love and miss dearly, who left us much too soon.

IN MEMORY 2011

My photographer, Jerry Jack, who was passionate about life and saw beauty in everything. He was so much fun and easy to be around when doing the photo shoot for the book. You are truly missed.

CPSIA information can be obtained
at www.ICGtesting.com
Printed in the USA
BVXC01n1333301014
372788BV00006B/28

* 9 7 8 0 9 8 4 0 7 5 0 0 3 *